LAB
Crayon

For Nina

AL YANKOVIC

When I Grow Up

Illustrations by WES HARGIS

HARPER
An Imprint of HarperCollinsPublishers

AMBER
LORI
Cc
Dd
MATT
WILL

I waited so long for the hours to pass,
But soon it was noon there in Mrs. Krupp's class.
And Thursday at noon, as I'm sure you know well,
Is the time of the week when we do show-and-tell.

And *this* week the subject—so special to me—
Was "When I grow up, what am I gonna be?"
That's something I'd really been thinking about,
And I just couldn't wait to let all those thoughts out.

So when Mrs. Krupp said, "Who's ready to share?"
You can guess who was there with his hand in the air!
I raised *both* my hands just as high as they'd go,
And I bounced up and down and then—what do you know?
Well, Mrs. Krupp picked me—yes, *me*—to go first!
Oh, I was so happy I thought I would burst!

I proudly stood up and began my oration
Concerning my choice for a future vocation.

"Esteemed friends and colleagues and dear Mrs. Krupp,
I know what I'm gonna be when I grow up . . .

Why, I'll be the greatest chef you've ever seen.
The world will go crazy for my *haute cuisine*!
I'll tantalize taste buds with my rigatoni
Sautéed with black truffles and pickled baloney
Surrounded by kumquats and candied pigs feet
Topped with shrimp-flavored lollipops—*bon appétit*!

My walls will be filled with awards that I've gotten
For toast-on-a-stick and my Twinkies *au gratin*.
My kitchen will be the most famous in France,
So make reservations twelve years in advance!
There's no doubt about it—I'm certain, you see—
A world-renowned chef is what I'm gonna be."

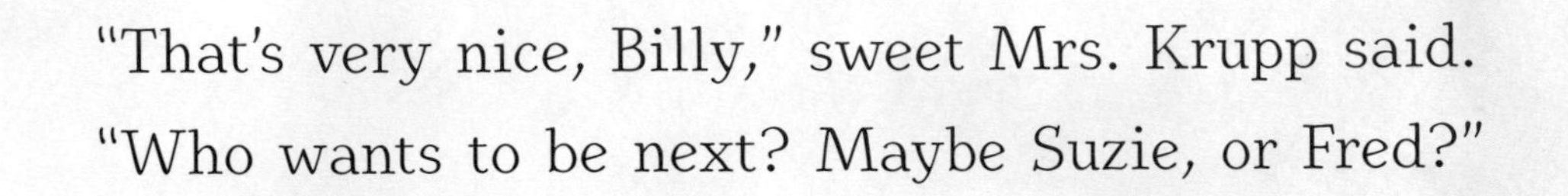

"That's very nice, Billy," sweet Mrs. Krupp said.
"Who wants to be next? Maybe Suzie, or Fred?"

I said, "Hold the phone now, I haven't departed.
Hang on to your seats, 'cause I'm just getting started!

See, maybe instead I could be a *snail trainer*!
Man, that would be awesome! Why, that's a no-brainer!
I'll teach all my snails to do really neat tricks:
They'll play dead, roll over, and even fetch sticks!
Of course, all the sticks will come back two years later . . .
But working with snails—I mean, what could be greater?
They'll do any stunt that I like—holy moley!—
I'll train 'em to pedal a bike really *slowwwly*,
Then jump (I mean *ooze*) through a huge ring of fire,
And crawl at a snail's pace across a high wire,
Then finish by writing my name with their trails!
That's right, I'll be *Billy: The Master of Snails*!

B
B
Billy

Or else maybe I'll be the lathe operator
Who makes the hydraulic torque wrench calibrator
Which fine-tunes the wrench that's specifically made
To retighten the nuts on the lateral blade
That's directly beneath the main radial sockets
Inside cooling systems on X-14 rockets—
And since this profession's as cool as can be,
Well, who would be better to do it than me?

Say, here's an idea—perhaps just for laughs
I might make my living by milking giraffes!
It's oh-so-*cliché* to get milk from a cow,
And I bet all those cows need a break anyhow.
Imagine me milking way up in the air!
I'd use a tall ladder instead of a chair—"

"What? Milking giraffes?" Mrs. Krupp said. "Oh, please!"
I countered, "How else could we make giraffe *cheese*?
Now don't interrupt me, I'm not really through yet,
There's still lots of stuff that I'm planning to do yet!

'Cause maybe I'll be a gorilla masseuse . . .

Or an artist who sculpts out of chocolate mousse

Or a rodeo clown or a movie director
Or maybe professional pickle inspector
Or big sumo wrestler or hedge-fund investor
Or smelly pit-sniffing deodorant tester

Or I'll be an expert on nuclear fission
Or else a foot model or friendly mortician
Or waiter or skater or master debater
Or dinosaur-dusting museum curator
Or TV repairman or sidewalk sign waver
Or part-time assistant tarantula shaver—"

And that's about when Mrs. Krupp said, "Now, Billy.
Please make up your mind—this is getting quite silly!
Which one of those things are you going to choose?"
I shuffled around, and I looked at my shoes . . .

And finally I said, "My great-grandfather Bob's
Been a whole lot of things, had a whole bunch of jobs:
A butcher, a barber, a bellman, a bouncer,
A telephone psychic and bingo announcer.
You know what? He just turned a hundred and three,
And he's still not quite sure what *he* wants to be!

See, I'm only eight now, so frankly I'm hopin'
You'll cut me some slack if I leave options open.
Let's just wait and find out what my future brings—
Hey, I might have time to do *all* of those things!"

And then the bell rang and we all went to lunch,
And as I was sipping my pineapple punch,

I pondered professions that I'd like to enter
Like brave firefighter or crazy inventor . . .

Or maybe—just *maybe* now—when I grow up,
I can be a great teacher like dear Mrs. Krupp.

TeacHer Billy
FOR MRS KRUPP
LOVE BILLY

When I Grow Up

www.harpercollinschildrens.com

Library of Congress Cataloging-in-Publication Data is available.
ISBN 978-0-06-192691-4

Typography by Dana Fritts
11 12 13 14 15 LP/LPR 10 9 8 7 6 5 4 3
❖
First Edition